ROY KANE
TV DETECTIVE

This edition published 2008
First published 1998 by
A & C Black Publishers Ltd
38 Soho Square, London, W1D 3HB

www.acblack.com

ISBN 978-0-7136-8629-6

A CIP catalogue for this book is available from the British Library.

This book is produced using paper that is made from wood grown in managed, sustainable forests. It is natural, renewable and recyclable. The logging and manufacturing processes conform to the environmental regulations of the country of origin.

Printed and bound in China by C&C Offset Printing Co.,Ltd.

ROY KANE TV DETECTIVE

Steve Bowkett

Illustrated by David Burroughs

A & C Black • London

Thursday October 14th, 6.42 p.m.
Clayton City Museum had been closed since five that afternoon. The only person left in the building was Alex Harvey, the Museum Director…

Suddenly, the alarm went off.

Sergeant Greg Mulholland and Officer Brad Michalik were first on the scene. They found Alex Harvey inside, pacing up and down.

I don't understand it. I just don't understand it!
Take it easy, sir. Brad, go and check to see if anything is missing. Then report back here.
Yes, sir.

Oh, don't bother doing that. I know exactly what's missing. There's only one thing any burglar would want to steal from here. Come on, I'll show you.

The three men walked through shadowy corridors and galleries until they reached a new exhibition.
THE MAGIC OF ANCIENT EGYPT

Alex Harvey walked quickly past the displays, leading the police officers to a large, glittering showcase. It was empty.

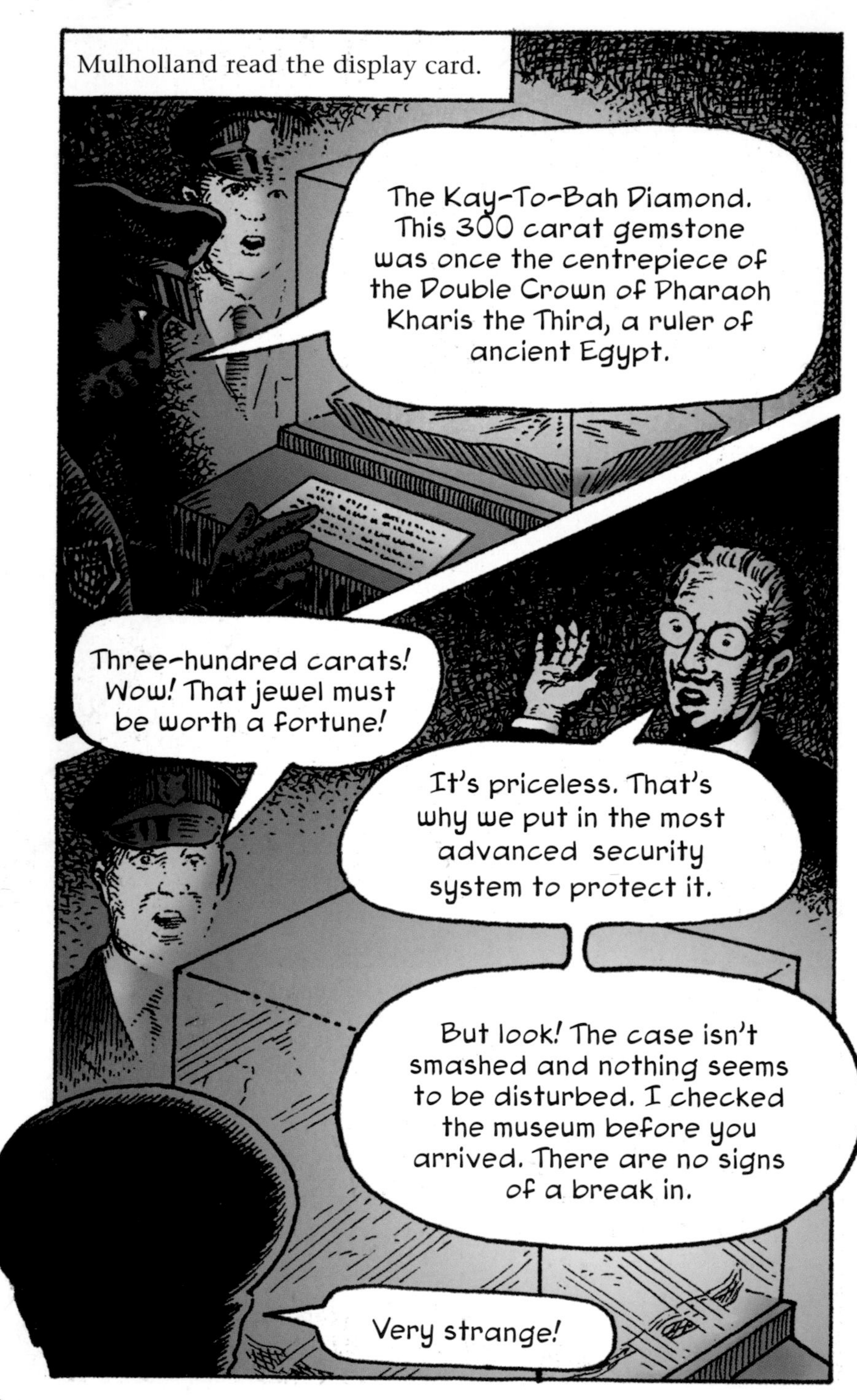
Mulholland read the display card.
The Kay-To-Bah Diamond. This 300 carat gemstone was once the centrepiece of the Double Crown of Pharaoh Kharis the Third, a ruler of ancient Egypt.
Three-hundred carats! Wow! That jewel must be worth a fortune!
It's priceless. That's why we put in the most advanced security system to protect it.
But look! The case isn't smashed and nothing seems to be disturbed. I checked the museum before you arrived. There are no signs of a break in.
Very strange!

What am I going to do? The Kay-To-Bah Diamond doesn't even belong to the museum. It's on loan from Mr Carmody.
Magnus Carmody, the billionaire?
Yes. He'll close us down! He'll have me fired!
Brad, get on the phone to Roy Kane, TV Detective. If there's anyone who can crack this case, it's him!

CCTV Studios, 7.05 p.m.
Mulholland and Michalik had arranged to meet Roy Kane at his TV studio. They arrived just as Roy was finishing his latest episode of Kane on the Case.
N THE CASE
CCTV
...And so that's how the case was solved. Who would have believed that a humble scientist would have used his latest invention, an all-purpose glue, to turn to a life of crime?
But one thing's for sure. Dario Menzel, The Human Spider, came unstuck in the end. This is Roy Kane wishing you well until the next episode of "Kane on the Case" Thank you and good night!

Mulholland explained about the robbery at the museum.

"So you're telling me the alarm went off after the diamond was taken?" Roy said, frowing. "And there was no forced entry... Have you checked the security camera video?"

Mulholland shook his head. "Not yet," he said.

"Leave that to me," said Roy. He took out a notepad and scribbled an address.

Jez Macintosh's house, 8.54 p.m.
Jez had used his skills to help Roy on a number of past cases. But could he help him now? Roy's other assistant, Vicki Stand, was also there. They listened as Roy filled them in on the details of the museum robbery.

So, no one saw anyone enter or leave the museum?
There's nothing on those security videos.
What about the videos from the Jewel Room itself? Have you looked at them yet?
I took a quick look just before Vicki got here. Check this out!

Jez pushed a button and a picture of the Egyptian Jewel Room in the museum glowed on a nearby screen.

Now look, right there! For just a few seconds, a strange mist covers the Kay-To-Bah Diamond.
When the mist fades away, the jewel is gone!
Yes, but that doesn't help us.

It might. I can process the footage to filter out the fog.

Jez worked at the keyboard for a few minutes.
OK, let's run it again.
A second later...
EEEEEEEEEEEEE
Well, at least we know it wasn't aliens from outer space.
But it's pretty advanced trickery all the same. I think we need some technical advice.
There's a magician playing at the Deangate Theatre – Doctor Praetorius. Maybe he can help us.
Good idea. Jez, will you carry on working on the security video. Vicki and I will go and see if this Doctor Praetorius is all he's cracked up to be.

CHAPTER TWO

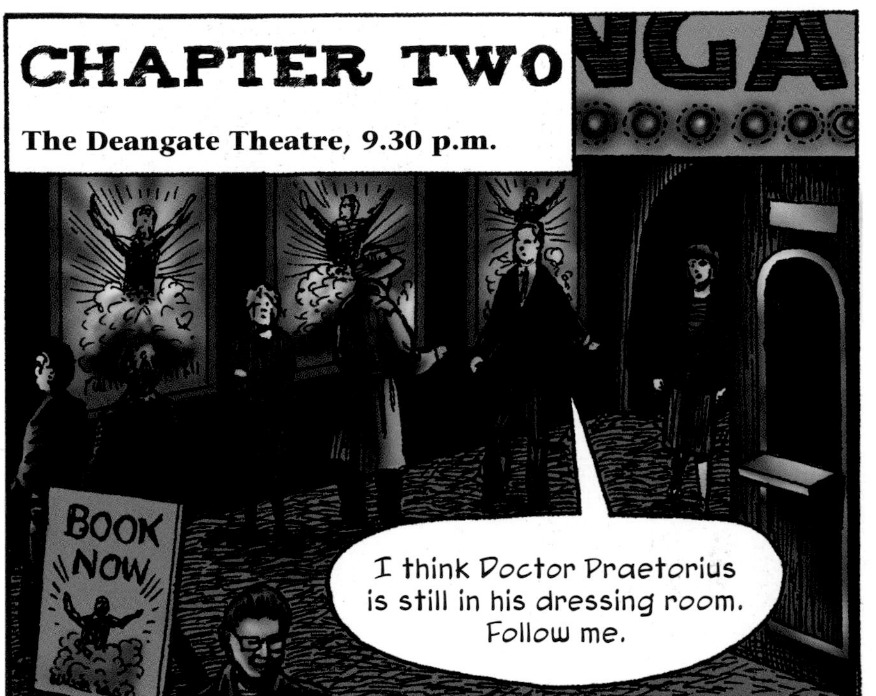
The Deangate Theatre, 9.30 p.m.
BOOK NOW
I think Doctor Praetorius is still in his dressing room. Follow me.

I've seen Praetorius on TV. Some of the things he does are amazing!
MR ALBERT WATTS
DR. PRAETORIUS
KNOCK!
Come in.
Clever trickery, Vicki. That's all it is.

Roy and Vicki stepped inside. The room was an Aladdin's cave of treasures filled with props and equipment Doctor Praetorius used to perform his mind-boggling illusions. The magician and his wife and assistant, Lisa, were busy tidying up after the show.

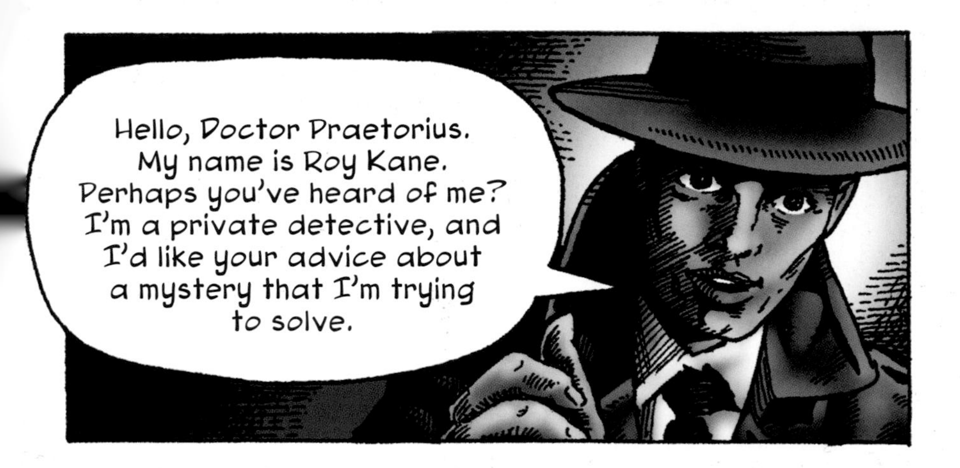

Roy explained about the missing Kay-To-Bah Diamond, and the trickery that had seemingly been used to steal it.

"I'm sorry, Mr Kane," said Praetorius when Roy had finished. "But I can't help you."

Roy and Vicki drove back across town to see how Jez had been getting on…
Well, even if he couldn't help us, I still think his magic is amazing.
Call it detective's intuition, but I think there is more to Doctor Praetorius than meets the eye.
Surely you'd expect one of the world's greatest magicians to be a little mysterious?

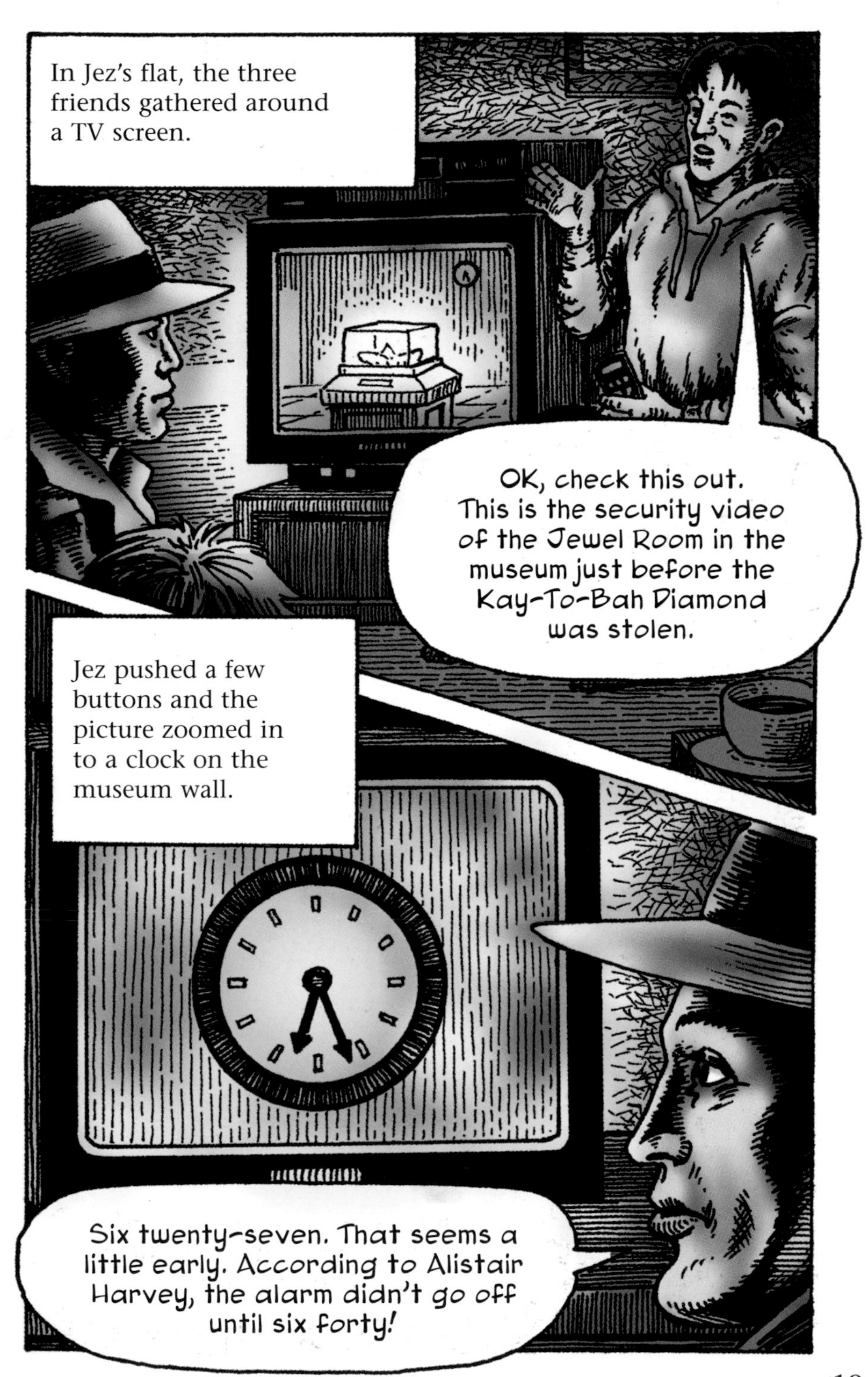
In Jez's flat, the three friends gathered around a TV screen.
OK, check this out. This is the security video of the Jewel Room in the museum just before the Kay-To-Bah Diamond was stolen.
Jez pushed a few buttons and the picture zoomed in to a clock on the museum wall.
Six twenty-seven. That seems a little early. According to Alistair Harvey, the alarm didn't go off until six forty!

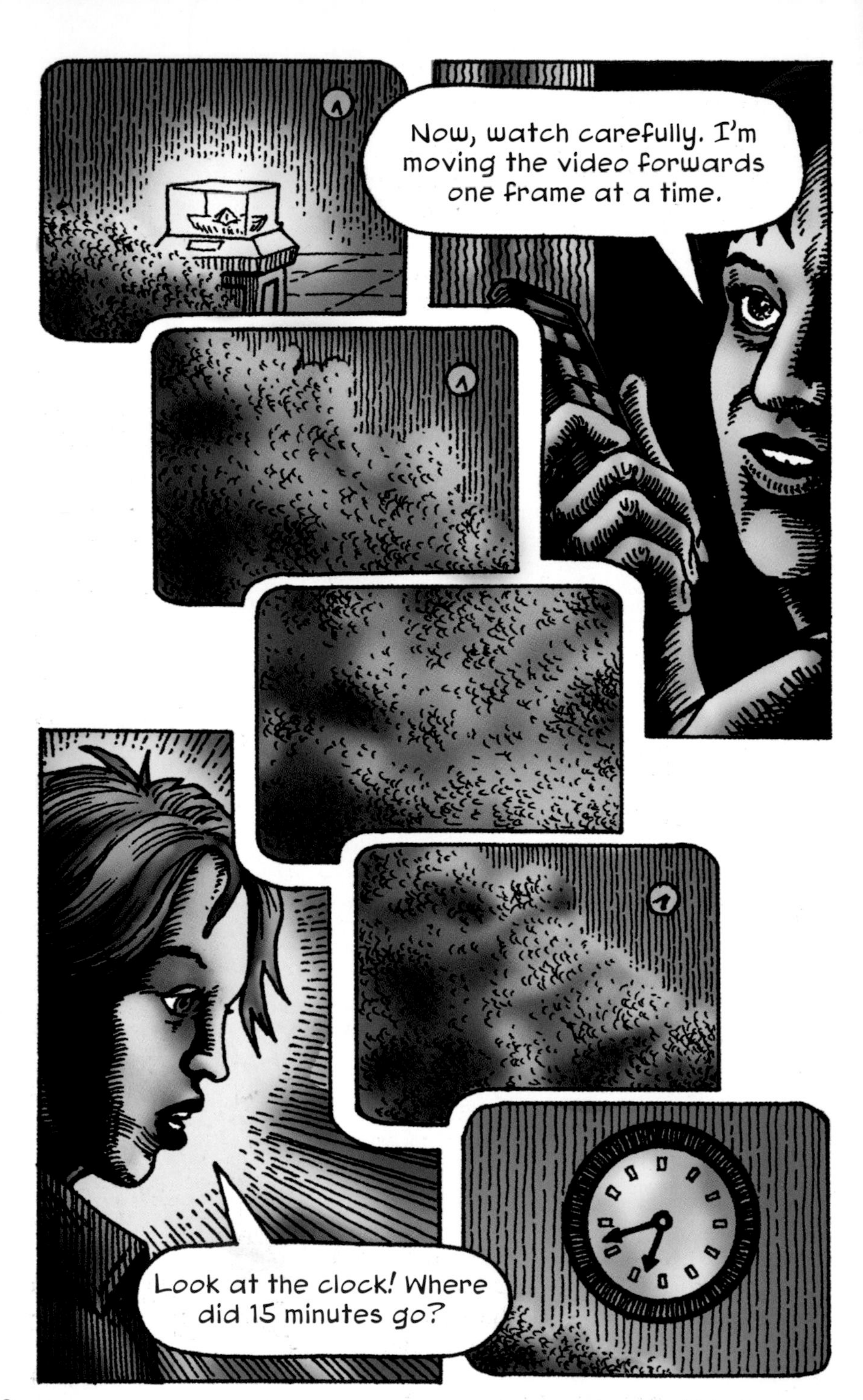
Now, watch carefully. I'm moving the video forwards one frame at a time.
Look at the clock! Where did 15 minutes go?

Fifteen minutes! The time it took the thief to turn off the alarm, open the case, and make off with the diamond! It didn't happen in just one second! This was all a trick, an illusion.

It always comes down to technology in the end. But there's more. See! There's the thief!

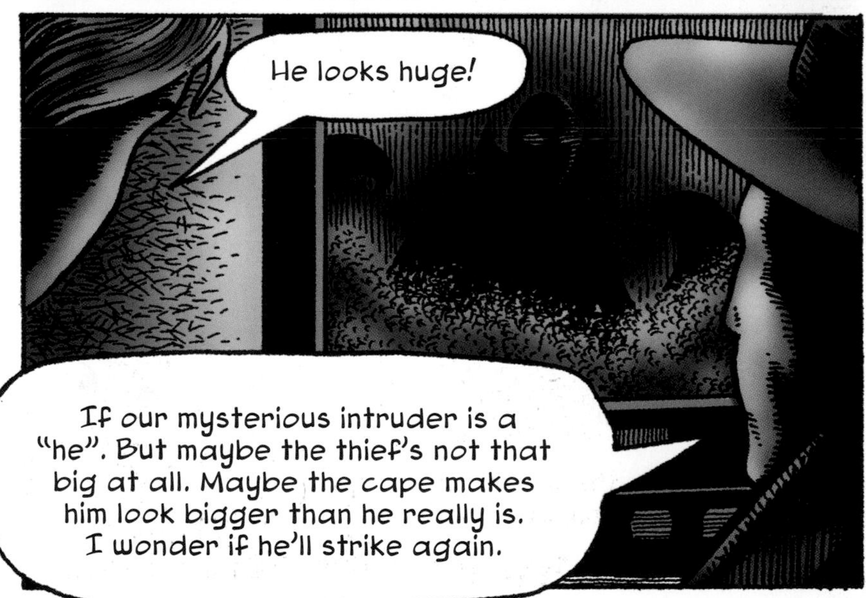
He looks huge!
If our mysterious intruder is a "he". But maybe the thief's not that big at all. Maybe the cape makes him look bigger than he really is. I wonder if he'll strike again.

Saturday, October 16th, 11.25 p.m.
At a downtown warehouse, a security guard carried out his routine checks. A shadowy figure watched him from a distance.
Suddenly, the building burst into flames!
WHOOSH!
Aargh!

Hey!

What the...

Fire! Police! Quick!
The building - it's on fire!
SECURITY

Emergency services were quickly on the scene. Roy and his team arrived soon afterwards.
So, what's going on?
We've got the blaze under control now. But the contents of the warehouse have been completely destroyed. There's not much doubt this was done on purpose!

We've found an empty petrol can and traces of a device that started the fire. I've got men up on the roof hunting for clues. Someone was spotted up there before the fire started.
Any chance we could take a look up there, chief?
Sure, follow me.

They climbed up to the roof and began to explore. After a few minutes, Vicki saw a strange object lying in the rubble.
Roy! Jez! I've found something.

Don't get too close, Vicki. It might be dangerous.
Vicki!
PSSSSSSSSSS
Aargh!

Roy launched himself at the shadowy figure...

WHUMP!
...but the cape was empty!

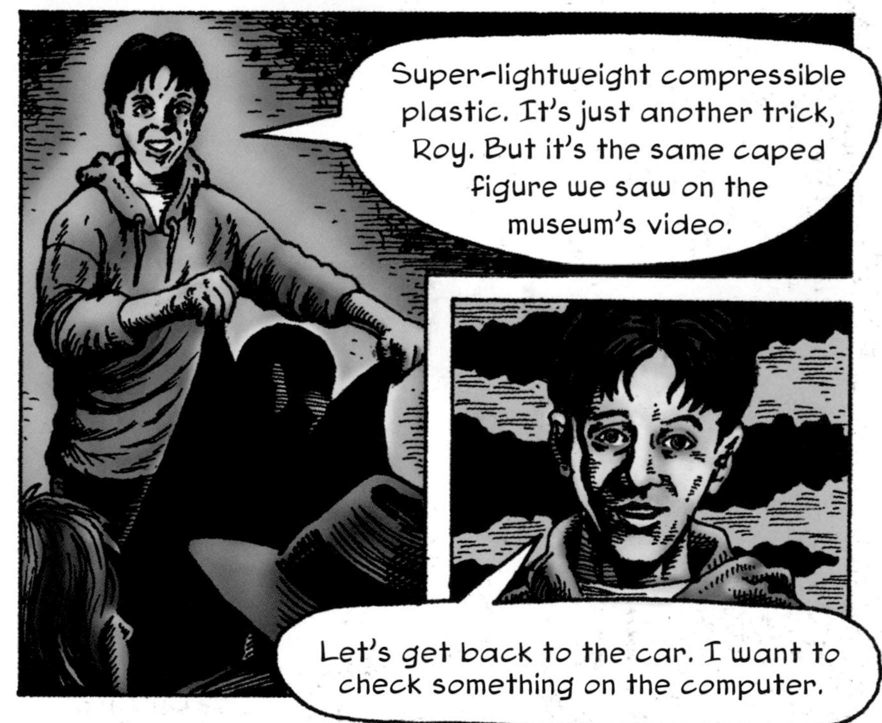
Super-lightweight compressible plastic. It's just another trick, Roy. But it's the same caped figure we saw on the museum's video.
Let's get back to the car. I want to check something on the computer.

Soon after...
Ah, here we are. Warehouse and Storage, Clayton West Sector, Wharfside. Well, what do you know?
What have you found?

I bet I know what he's found. That the warehouse is owned by Magnus Carmody.
You're right. This whole block belongs to a company called Mega Commodities. The director of that company is our friend Carmody the billionaire, who is also the owner of the stolen diamond!
Like I said, there are some clever people around...

Nearby…
Attention, all units! A prowler has been seen near the river on Eastbank. He is heading towards the city centre. Close in and wait for further orders. Attention, all units...
POLIC
Hey, Roy. It sounds like we might have your man.
POLICE
We're on our way. Get on the phone to Mulholland and tell him to meet us there.
Mulholland here. OK, copy that, suspect sighted on Eastbank. Over and out. Brad... step on it! We're only a few blocks away.

Up ahead, Sarge! Do you see that?
He's turned down an alley towards River Row. We can head him off. Quick!
As they rounded the corner, the officers were blinded by the headlights from another car.
POLICE
SCREEECH
What the... What does that fool think he's doing?

He's on our side of the road! The idiot he's –
Look out!
SCREEECH!!
RRIPP!!
CRASH!

CHAPTER THREE
Roy, Vicki, and Jez were the first on the scene. Luckily, no one was badly hurt.
Run through it again for me, would you, Greg?
There's no more to add. We saw the caped figure turn into an alley. I thought we could inercept him at the far end.

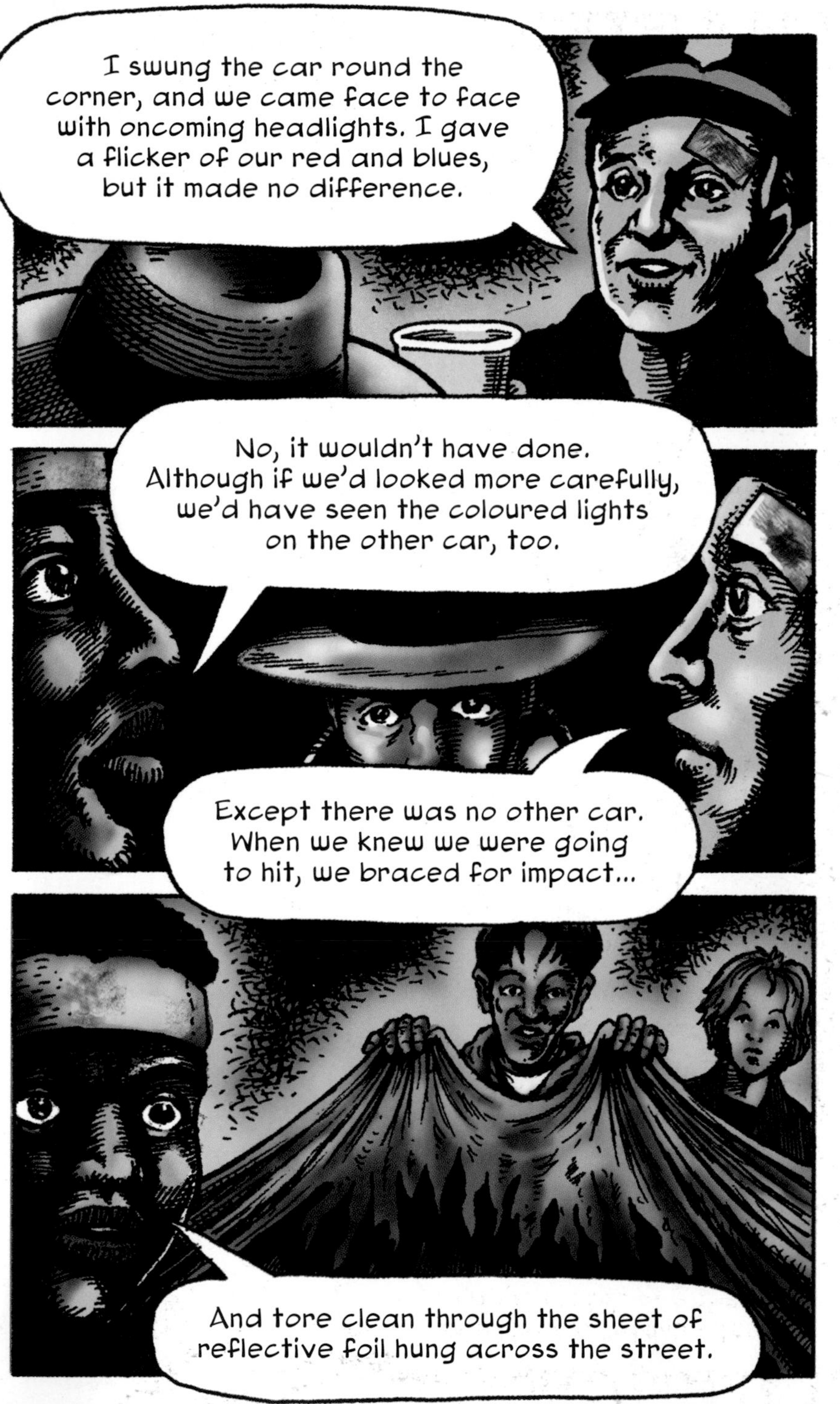
I swung the car round the corner, and we came face to face with oncoming headlights. I gave a flicker of our red and blues, but it made no difference.
No, it wouldn't have done. Although if we'd looked more carefully, we'd have seen the coloured lights on the other car, too.
Except there was no other car. When we knew we were going to hit, we braced for impact...
And tore clean through the sheet of reflective foil hung across the street.

It was pure bad luck that the front offside wheel hit the kerb.

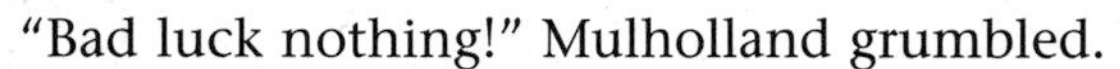
"Bad luck nothing!" Mulholland grumbled.

If you ask me, this trick was carefully planned. The caped figure put up that mirror sheet earlier, to fool us. By running down that alley, he lured us into following him.
You're right, Greg. This whole thing is getting very dangerous. And it keeps coming back to clever trickery...

So, do we grill Doctor Praetorius again?
All in good time. First I want to meet the other player in the game, Magnus Carmody. We'll go to see him first thing on Monday morning.

Monday, October 18th, 9.10 a.m.
All right. Thanks. I appreciate that.
Carmody's secretary has booked an appointment for us to see him in half an hour. We're meeting him out at Pen Flats – he's got some kind of development project there. Let's get going.

Half an hour later, they pulled up to a large portacabin. Huge, skeletal structures towered upwards all around them. Roy knocked at the door and they went inside.

Hello. I'm Roy Kane, and this is my assistant, Vicki Stand. We have an appointment with–

I'm Magnus Carmody. What can I do for you?

Roy ran through the details that had brought them to see him; the theft of the Kay-To-Bah Diamond, and the arson attack on Carmody's warehouse.

Mr Kane, over the years I've made many enemies. I'm rich and successful....
And modest...
To get where I am today, sometimes I've had to be ruthless. There are plenty of people who would love to see me ruined.
What about Albert Watts?

Albert Watts? Now there's a name I haven't heard in a long time. He and I went to school together. He was a gutless coward, who ran away from every fight.

What does Albert Watts have to do with my missing diamond and my warehouse going up in flames?

Maybe nothing at all. We're just being thorough. You see, we're professionals, just like you are, Carmody, and I fully intend to catch this criminal, whoever he is...
Soon after...
It sounded a bit like you were threatening him, Roy.
Not really. But a veiled threat won't hurt – it'll give Carmody something to think about.
So, what's our next move?
I'd like you to check out what Carmody said about Albert Watts. Meanwhile, I'll book us a couple of tickets for Praetorius' next show. I want to see just how clever he really is.

The Deangate Theatre, 8.15 p.m.
Later that day, Roy met Vicki at the theatre.
“Listen to this, Roy,” said Vicki, full of excitement. “I spoke to a teacher at Carmody’s old high school. She remembers both him and Watts from her first year of teaching.”
SKETS
And they hated each other, right?
How did you know?
Detective’s intuition...
Apparantly they really hated each other. Carmody was a notorious bully and often picked on Watts. But Watts knew tricks and magic even back then, and used his skills to make Carmody look like a fool.

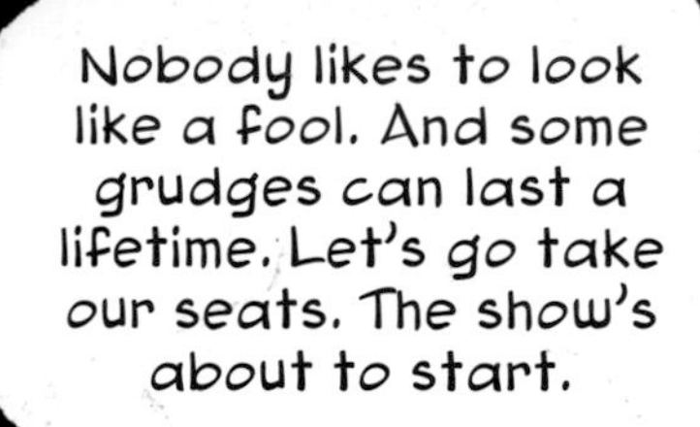
Nobody likes to look like a fool. And some grudges can last a lifetime. Let's go take our seats. The show's about to start.

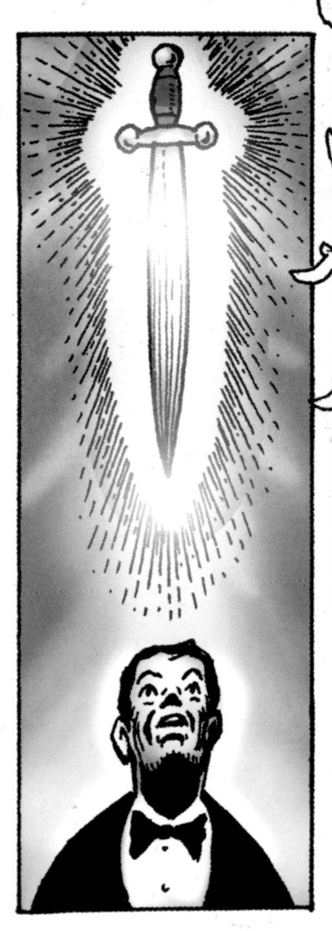

Wow! That was brilliant!

Yes, great show.

But there aren't that many people here tonight... I wonder why?

Right, let's get backstage and have a snoop around. No need to talk to anyone. Just see if you can pick up some gossip, any details that might help us.

Roy walked round the back of the theatre to the stage door and mingled with the fans waiting to catch a glimpse of Doctor Praetorius. Meanwhile, Vicki went to the dressing rooms. Ther was a heated argument going on.

It isn't my fault if people aren't coming to see us! My act is the best there is! I'm the great Doctor Praetorius!

The door slammed shut. Vicki ducked behind a curtain as the theatre manager stormed by When he'd gone, she turned to sneak away but there, standing right in front of her, was Doctor Praetorius.

CHAPTER FOUR
Ohhh! What happened?

But - how? You're in two places at once!
What's going on?
Roy! It's Praetorius!

I seem to have startled your assistant. She fainted when she saw me.

There's really nothing to be frightened of.

It's a trick we often use in our act. I "disappear", then miraculoulsy reappear somewhere else. But it's Lisa in disguise.

May I?

This mask is made of rubber and looks exactly like skin. Simple, but brilliant, Mr Watts.

That's Lisa's expertise.
I studied art and design at college. I specialised in human portraiture.

She could have made a name for herself as a sculptess – but married me instead and devoted her life to our act.

Well, it fooled me!

The mask is a trade secret. Albert and I would not want you to reveal it to anyone.

We won't do anything to ruin the illusion, Mrs Watts. Not if we can help it...

A short while later, in Roy's car...

Do you still suspect Praetorius of being the caped stranger?
I'm keeping my options open, but the evidence is stacked against him.

So, we need to find out more.
Exactly - which is why, tomorrow morning, I'd like you to dig a bit deeper into Albert Watts's past. And find out all you can about Lisa Watts, too.
Anything else?
Yes! Get hold of any further records on Magnus Carmody. We all have skeletons in the cupboard, and I want to know exactly what Carmody's are!
Slave driver!

Pen Flats Site Office, 10.27 p.m.
Later that night, Magnus Carmody worked at his construction site. Everyone else had gone home.

As Carmody reached his car, the darkness suddenly was pierced by a brilliant beam of light. A huge shadow suddenly appeared out of nowhere!

You have haunted me, Carmody! You have destroyed me!
Wh- what do you mean?
Now I am going to destroy you!
You ruined my life, Carmody! Now I will ruin yours!
What have I done?
Who are you?
Aargh! Get away!

Carmody ran to his car. He revved the engine and sped away.

A traffic patrol car was parked on the highway watching for speeding motorists.

POLICE
The police – that's all I need!
Suddenly, a cloud of mist billowed up inside Carmody's car, and out of it loomed the face of Death!
No! No!
SCREEEE

SMASH!

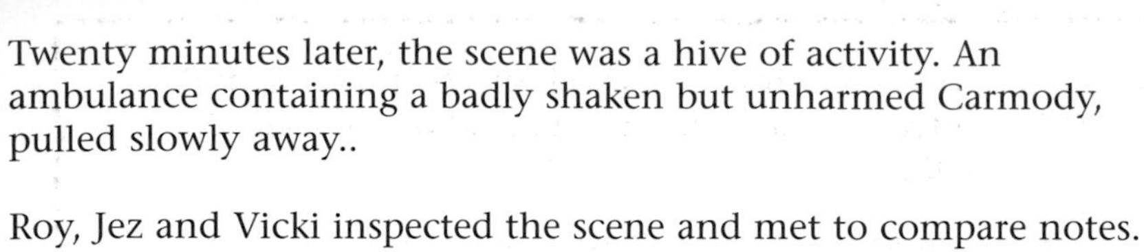
Twenty minutes later, the scene was a hive of activity. An ambulance containing a badly shaken but unharmed Carmody, pulled slowly away..
Roy, Jez and Vicki inspected the scene and met to compare notes. A small, box-like device had been found.

This is turning into quite a night.
So now it's attempted murder. You figured out that little device yet, Jez?
It's ingenious. Watch.
POL

Jez stepped back and flipped a switch on the box. A cloud of mist instantly rose up around him. And out of the mist appeared the figure of Death.

What we have here is a holographic projector coupled with a gas cylinder which produces the mist. It's brilliant!

CLICK!

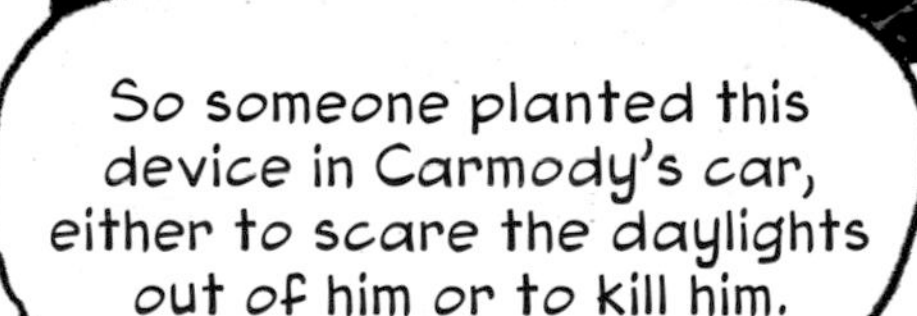

So someone planted this device in Carmody's car, either to scare the daylights out of him or to kill him.

And it nearly succeeded.

Another fancy illusion. I think it's time that Albert Watts was pulled in for questioning. I'll ring Chief Inspector Lane and set it up.

Later that night, a patrol car pulled up outside the Watts' smart, suburban house.
POLIC
Oh! Is there something wrong, officers?
We'd like to ask your husband a few questions, ma'am.
Down at the station.
But why? What's going on?
If you wouldn't mind letting your husband know, Mrs Watts.
Albert! Albert, the police are here.

A few seconds later,
Mr Watts appeared.
I don't understand. My wife says you want to question me. Why?

Sir, we simply need to ask where you were tonight, and one or two other matters. It's just routine.

I was about to go to bed. Really, this is most unusual...
What the...?

CHAPTER FIVE

Thursday, October 19th, 7.42 a.m.
Clayton City Museum.

A few minutes later...
What do you mean "the evidence is circumstantial"? Watts was caught red-handed with the diamond!
Come on. You told me about the look on Watts's face. You said he was as surprised as the rest of you. That diamond could have been planted.
Besides, you've been questioning Watts all night. Has he confessed, yet?

No chance. He says he knows nothing about it.

Well, maybe he's telling the truth! Let's wait and see.

A short time later, Roy and Vicki arrived at Jez's apartment.
What's the news on Carmody then, Vicki?

Well, Watts and Carmody not only went to the same high school, they also studied at Clayton University together. And it was there they met Lisa Harris, who would later become Mrs Watts.

So?
So the grudge between Watts and Carmody grew worse and worse. They both liked Lisa. She married Watts and moved away. Carmody started up his company and grew rich...

And now Watts and Lisa have returned to Clayton, bought a home, and plan to settle.

Carmody is getting tormented all over again...

OK. Here's another connection...

You asked me to cross-check Carmody's companies with ticket sales at the theatres where Doctor Praetorius has been appearing...

Praetorius' audiences have been small...
But the figures say ticket sales are good!

"Do you see what's been going on?" Roy asked his two friends. "Carmody has been buying up tickets for Praetorius's shows, so no one else can buy them. But not using the seats."
His plan was to destroy Watts' reputation, by creating small audiences. And maybe–
Maybe by planting the Kay-To-Bah Diamond in Watts' coat!
You mean, Carmody stole the diamond from himself?
Perhaps. But I think the first person we need to talk to is the manager of the Deangate Theatre.

They drove to the theatre...
STAFF

Mr Watson. Do you have a moment?

What do you want?

Sir, we want to ask you about the block-buying of tickets...

I don't know anything...

And I also wonder if you "don't know anything" about a rather expensive diamond, Mr Watson?

No!
Did Magnus Carmody pay you to plant that diamond in Albert Watts' coat pocket?

No, that wasn't me! I had nothing to do with that!
Stop him!

Suddenly, everything went dark. A moment later, Vicki and Roy were dazzled by an eerie spotlight. Mist billowed up, seemingly from nowhere. Then, a terrifying figure cast its shadow across the stage.

HA HA HA HA HA HA HA HA HA HA

Let's see how he likes this!

THUD!

The shape of the caped stranger fell empty to the floor. Above the stage, a hand reached out and dropped one of the spotlights.
Roy! Look out!
That was close! Thanks, Vicki. I owe you one.
Don't mention it. Shall we go and find Watson?
No, he's not important. There's something else I need to check.

Roy took out his phone and keyed in a number. A moment later the voice of Magnus Carmody's secretary answered.
Hello. Roy Kane. I'd like to speak with Mr Carmody please. It's urgent.
I'll put you through.
Carmody, here.
CLICK!
Hmm, so Carter is not the caped figure.
Then who is?
At this moment, Vicki, your guess is as good as mine.

CHAPTER SIX

Tuesday, October 19th, 11.26 a.m.
Roy and Vicki met with Jez in a coffee shop not far from the Deangate Theatre.

You could have been killed, Roy!
The killer knows we're getting close. And since the trap was sprung at the theatre, it means he knows his way around there.

We know that the guy in the cape is not Albert Watts. He's still at the police station.

And we know it isn't Carmody. He was at work when you called.

So, if we rule out Carter, that leaves someone we don't know about yet... or Lisa Watts.
What!
OK, OK. It's just an idea.

But we're playing a dangerous game now. We can't afford to make a mistake. If we assume the killer plans to destroy Carmody, his Head Office is likely to be the next target.

Do we stake it out?
We don't know when the thief will strike next. I've got another plan.

1.19 p.m. Stage 1 of the plan.
Roy dropped Vicki off outside Watts's house.

Oh, Miss Stand. What do you want?

We have reason to believe that your life may be in danger. I've been asked to stay with you for your protection.

So, with Lisa Watts covered, if the caped figure shows up tonight, we'll know that she's in the clear.

Clever.

Now, let's get over to Carmody's office.

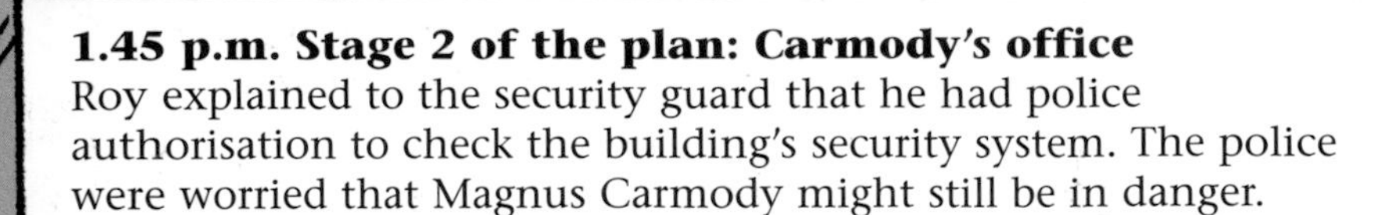

1.45 p.m. Stage 2 of the plan: Carmody's office
Roy explained to the security guard that he had police authorisation to check the building's security system. The police were worried that Magnus Carmody might still be in danger.

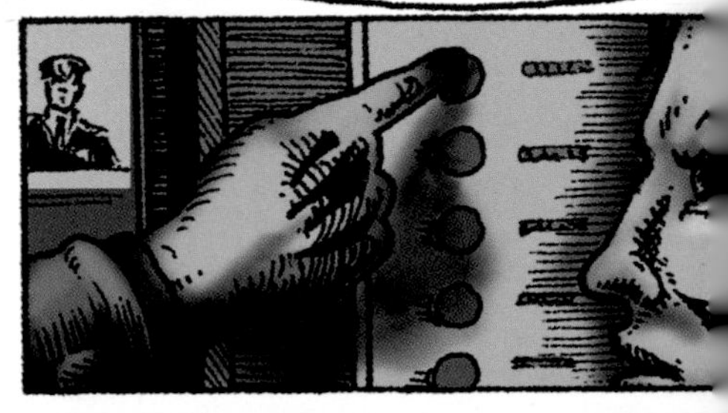

Is Mr Carmody in the building right now?
No, sir, but he's expected later.
OK, we'll speak with him then. Come on, Jez.

Great. Right, we'll set up a couple of our own cameras here, one in Carmody's office and another in the lobby.

When the cameras were in place, Roy and Jez returned to the car.
All right, Greg, thanks for letting me know.

That was Mulholland. Watts got himself a good lawyer and they've had to let him go. They're going to follow him. Anything going on?

Typical daytime TV, Roy. Real boring!
I'll call Vicki and see if she's OK.

Lisa checked that Vicki was unconcious, before hurrying from the house.

Back in Roy's car, Jez continued to monitor the security cameras on his computer. Everything was normal. Then suddenly, the building's cameras went out. Jeff checked his own cameras – they were still working. One of them showed a strange mist billowing into the lobby. The security guard had passed out.

Just as Roy took out his phone, it began to ring. Jeff watched the computer screen and saw Carmody pick up his phone, too.

Darling. It's me.
Albert's been released.
I'm coming for you now!
I'm coming for you now!

It's the thief!
I'm calling Vicki.

It was several minutes before Vicki answered her phone.
I don't know what happened, Roy, but Lisa Watts has disappeared!
OK, Vicki. Come over here now. We're going up to Carmody's office.

CHAPTER SEVEN

Roy and Jez hurried to the lobby of the building. They checked that the guard was all right, before taking the elevator to Carmody's office. In the outer room, they found his secretary unconscious. Inside Carmody's room, they discovered signs of a struggle.

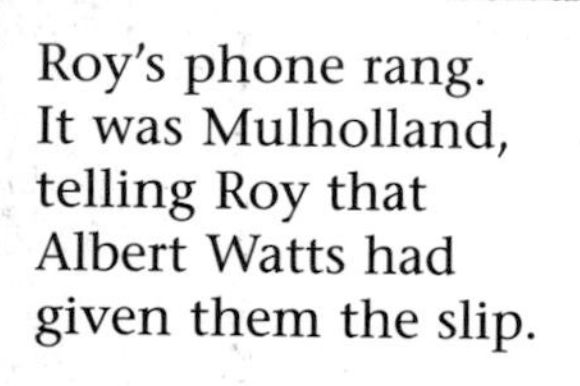
Roy's phone rang. It was Mulholland, telling Roy that Albert Watts had given them the slip.
Watts is sure to be heading this way. Because even if he isn't the killer, he knows who is.

Carmody reached the edge of the roof and peered down. Far below, police cars screeched to a halt and officers rushed into the building. Carmody turned around to try and find his way back.
Now, Carmody, now you'll pay. After all these years of hate, I have you!
I don't understand! What have I ever done to you?
You made fun of me. You tried to destroy my career. You even took my wife away.
Watts? It can't be you!

Why? Don't you think poor old Albert Watts is smart enough to trick you?

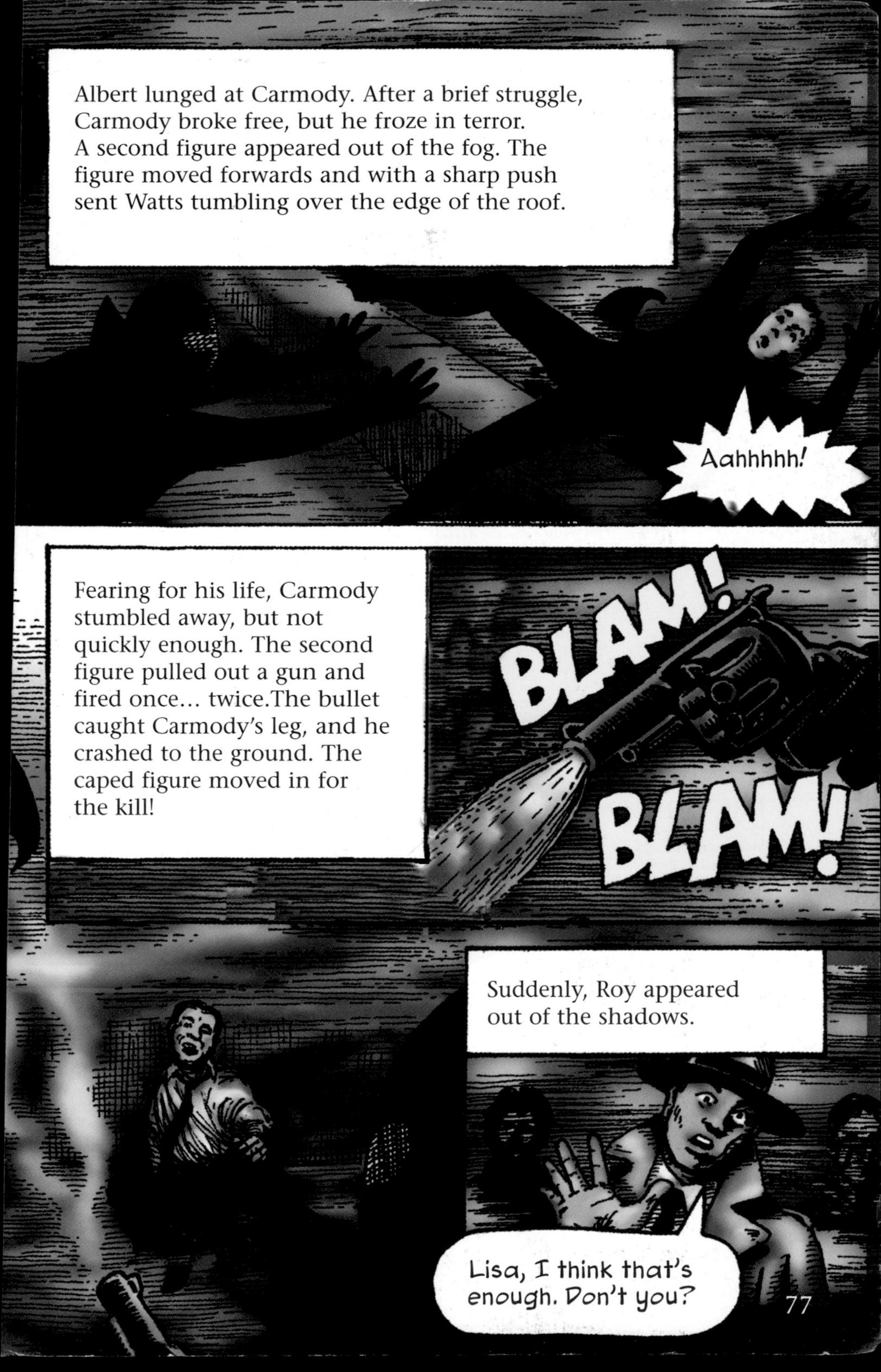
Albert lunged at Carmody. After a brief struggle, Carmody broke free, but he froze in terror. A second figure appeared out of the fog. The figure moved forwards and with a sharp push sent Watts tumbling over the edge of the roof.
Aahhhhh!
Fearing for his life, Carmody stumbled away, but not quickly enough. The second figure pulled out a gun and fired once... twice.The bullet caught Carmody's leg, and he crashed to the ground. The caped figure moved in for the kill!
BLAM!
BLAM!
Suddenly, Roy appeared out of the shadows.
Lisa, I think that's enough. Don't you?

After all they did? After all the empty promises?

Carmody just wanted me to be another thing that he owned.

What about Albert? Surely you loved him?

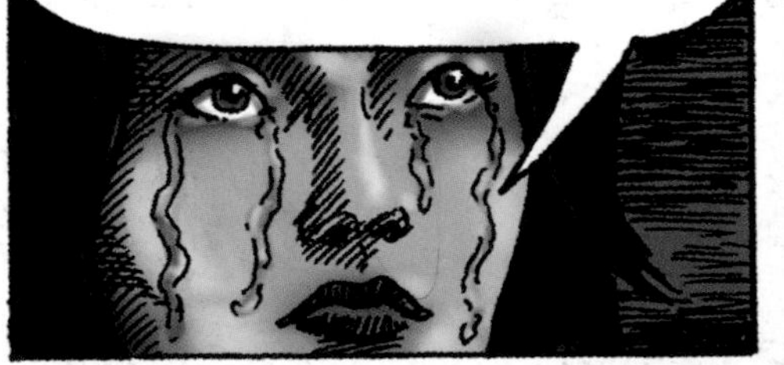
I envied his talent, but I grew to hate him for being nothing more than a stage magician. And I was his stupid little assistant. We could have done so much more!

The police officers led Lisa Watts away.
Suddenly, Roy and Jez heard a voice.
Help! Get me up from here!
Hold on, Mr Watts. We're coming!
CCTV Studios, 8.00 p.m.
. . . And so "Miss X," after being treated like a shadow, became a shadowy villain. She took revenge on the men who never allowed her to be in the spotlight herself.
KANE
ASE
This is Roy Kane, wishing you well until the next episode of "Kane on the Case". Thank you and good night!

APPLAUSE
OK, it's a wrap. Thanks, Roy, that was brilliant as usual.
Cheers, Doug.
I feel so sorry for Lisa.
Jealousy can do strange things to people. She envied Carmody his money and she envied Albert his fame. She thought her own talent was wasted.
Maybe Albert will wait for her...
What loyalty! And that's more important than money or fame, of course. True love conquers all!
Yeeuchh!